U0092983

# Matilda

## 解讀攻略

戴逸群——主編

林佳紋——編著

Joseph E. Schier——審閱

三民書局

國家圖書館出版品預行編目資料

Matilda 解讀攻略／戴逸群主編；林佳紋編著.——初
版一刷.——臺北市：三民，2020
面；　公分.——（閱讀成癮）

ISBN 978-957-14-6804-4 （平裝）
1. 英語 2. 讀本

805.18　　　　　　　　　　　　　　　109004844

閱讀成癮

# Matilda 解讀攻略

| | |
|---|---|
| 主　　　編 | 戴逸群 |
| 編 著 者 | 林佳紋 |
| 審　　　閱 | Joseph E. Schier |
| 責 任 編 輯 | 楊雅雯 |
| 美 術 編 輯 | 王立涵 |
| 封 面 繪 圖 | Steph Pai |
| 發 行 人 | 劉振強 |
| 出 版 者 | 三民書局股份有限公司 |
| 地　　　址 | 臺北市復興北路 386 號 ( 復北門市 ) |
| | 臺北市重慶南路一段 61 號 ( 重南門市 ) |
| 電　　　話 | (02)25006600 |
| 網　　　址 | 三民網路書店 https://www.sanmin.com.tw |
| 出 版 日 期 | 初版一刷 2020 年 5 月 |
| 書 籍 編 號 | S870470 |
| I S B N | 978-957-14-6804-4 |

三民書局

---
## 序
---

　　新課綱強調以「學生」為中心的教與學，注重學生的學習動機與熱情。而英文科首重語言溝通、互動的功能性，培養學生「自主學習」與「終身學習」的能力與習慣。小說「解讀攻略」就是因應新課綱的精神，在「英文小說中毒團隊」的努力下孕育而生。

　　一系列的「解讀攻略」旨在引導學生能透過原文小說的閱讀學習獨立思考，運用所學的知識與技能解決問題；此外也藉由廣泛閱讀進行跨文化反思，提升社會參與並培養國際觀。

　　「英文小說中毒團隊」由普高技高英文老師與大學教授組成，嚴選出主題多樣豐富、適合英文學習的原文小說。我們從文本延伸，設計多元有趣的閱讀素養活動，培養學生從讀懂文本到表達所思的英文能力。團隊秉持著改變臺灣英文教育的使命感，期許我們的努力能為臺灣的英文教育注入一股活水，翻轉大家對英文學習的想像！

戴逸群

# Contents

**Picture Credits**

All pictures in this publication are authorized for use by Shutterstock.

# The Reader of Books
## Pages 7-21

## Word Power

1. convince *v.* 說服
2. wash-out *n.* 徹底的失敗
3. stinker *n.* 討厭的人
4. extraordinary *adj.* 不平凡的
5. chatterbox *n.* 話匣子
6. librarian *n.* 圖書館員
7. be taken back 吃驚
8. devour *v.* 如饑似渴地閱讀
9. interfere *v.* 干涉
10. transport *v.* 使身臨其境

## Reading Comprehension

(　　) 1. What might the author enjoy writing for the stinkers in his class?
    (A) End-of-term reports.
    (B) Daily newspapers.
    (C) Science reports.
    (D) English essays.

(　　) 2. How did Matilda's parents treat her?
    (A) They cared about her so much and took good care of her.
    (B) They pushed her to join all kinds of competitions.
    (C) They always showed little interest in her.
    (D) They abused her and beat her.

(　　) 3. What was the first grown-up book that Mrs. Phelps recommended Matilda read?
    (A) *The Secret Garden* by Frances Hodgson Burnett.
    (B) *Pride and Prejudice* by Jane Austen.
    (C) *Jane Eyre* by Charlotte Brontë.
    (D) *Great Expectations* by Charles Dickens.

1. Matilda's hobby was reading, while that of her family was watching TV. Do you prefer reading or watching TV? State your reasons.

   _____

   _____

   _____

   _____

   _____

   _____

2. When Matilda got bored of only reading her mother's cookbooks and newspapers, what did she ask her father to do? Did her father grant or refuse her request? How did she solve the problem?

   _____

   _____

   _____

   _____

   _____

   _____

3. Mrs. Phelps was concerned about Matilda's safety when she knew Matilda came to the library alone without her parents' permission. However, she decided not to interfere. Do you think Mrs. Phelps's decision is right or wrong? Why?

   _____

   _____

   _____

   _____

   _____

   _____

 **A Book for U**

Imagine you are a YouTuber and you are introducing one of your favorite books to your audience. The following are the key points that you can use when you introduce the book.

**1** Briefly introduce the title of the book and the author.

**2** Summarize this book briefly and encourage your viewers to read it.

**3** What is the most impressive part in this book? What is the connection to your life?

**4** Who would you recommend this book to? What can they learn from this book?

# 2

## Mr. Wormwood, the Great Car Dealer &
## The Hat and the Superglue
## Pages 22–37

## Word Power

1. ignorant *adj.* 愚昧的
2. speedometer *n.* 車速表
3. dishonest *adj.* 不誠實的
4. nerve *n.* 膽量
5. soap opera *n.* 肥皂劇

6. resent *v.* 憤恨
7. cloakroom *n.* 衣帽間
8. gangster *n.* 歹徒
9. suspicion *n.* 懷疑
10. nasty *adj.* 令人不快的

## Reading Comprehension

(　) 1. What did Mr. Wormwood do with sawdust?
    (A) He mixed sawdust with the oil in the gear-box.
    (B) He used sawdust to polish old cars.
    (C) He used sawdust to reverse the mileage on old cars.
    (D) He put sawdust on the surface of tires.

(　) 2. How did Matilda's father react when she asked to eat supper at the dining table?
    (A) He was pleased and agreed to her request.
    (B) He also wanted to have his supper with Matilda at the dining table.
    (C) He got furious and yelled at her.
    (D) He didn't say anything about it.

(　) 3. How did Mrs. Wormwood help her husband get rid of the hat?
    (A) She washed the glue off the hat.
    (B) She pulled the hat off her husband's head.
    (C) She cut the hat and some hair off her husband's head.
    (D) She didn't do anything, and it slipped off her husband's head the next morning.

1. Matilda's father once said that no one ever got rich being honest. What was the difference between Matilda and her father? Do you think she has been influenced by her father? Why or why not?

_____

_____

_____

_____

_____

_____

2. If you were ignored or even insulted by your family members like Matilda was, what would you do?

_____

_____

_____

_____

_____

_____

3. Do you like to dine with your family at the dining table? What are the advantages and disadvantages of it?

_____

_____

_____

_____

_____

_____

## Michael's Diary

Imagine yourself as Michael and record in your diary the day when your father smugly taught you how to turn a car's mileage back to make money. However, your younger sister said it was dishonest and disgusting to make money in this way. Try to express your thoughts and feelings in your diary. Remember to use the past tense.

_____

_____

_____

_____

_____

_____

_____

_____

_____

# 3

# The Ghost
# Pages 38–48

## Word Power

1. sensible *adj.* 明智的
2. infuriate *v.* 激怒
3. snatch *v.* 搶奪
4. filth *n.* 汙垢
5. jealousy *n.* 嫉妒

6. chimney *n.* 煙囪
7. spooky *adj.* 幽靈般的
8. red-handed *adj.* 現行犯的
9. brandish *v.* （威脅地）揮舞
10. grumpy *adj.* 脾氣不好的

## Reading Comprehension

(　　) 1. Which of Matilda's friends lent Matilda a parrot?
    (A) Tom.
    (B) Tim.
    (C) Fred.
    (D) Frank.

(　　) 2. Which two phrases could the parrot say?
    (A) "Hello" and "All right."
    (B) "Hullo" and "Rattle my bones."
    (C) "Shut up" and "Come on."
    (D) "There it is" and "Save us."

(　　) 3. What did Matilda's father grab as a weapon when he thought there were some burglars in the house?
    (A) A golf-club.
    (B) A poker from the fireplace.
    (C) A table-lamp.
    (D) A knife.

1. Napoleon once said that the only sensible thing to do when you are attacked is to counterattack. What do you think Napoleon meant by saying so? Do you agree with it? Why or why not?

_____

_____

_____

_____

_____

_____

2. Do you believe in the existence of ghosts? Have you ever had any supernatural experiences?

_____

_____

_____

_____

_____

_____

3. When Matilda returned the parrot to her friend, she lied to him about what she had done with the parrot. What might be the reason she lied about it? Have you ever lied to a friend? How did you feel about it at the time?

_____

_____

_____

_____

_____

_____

## Problem and Solution

Let's explore the world of Matilda. Answer the following four questions to learn more about Matilda.

 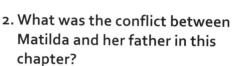

1. What do you know about Matilda?

2. What was the conflict between Matilda and her father in this chapter?

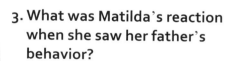 

3. What was Matilda's reaction when she saw her father's behavior?

4. How did Matilda solve her problem?

# Arithmetic
## Pages 49–55

## Word Power

1. arithmetic *n.* 算數
2. run rings around sb 遙遙領先某人
3. be obliged to 被迫去做⋯
4. civil *adj.* 有禮貌的
5. obediently *adv.* 服從地

6. diddle *v.* 騙取
7. high finance *n.* 大筆金額的財務
8. stiffen *v.* 變僵硬
9. exhausted *adj.* 筋疲力竭的

## Reading Comprehension

( ) 1. How much time did Mr. Wormwood spend working out the math problem he asked his son?
    (A) Less than 10 seconds.
    (B) Less than 5 minutes.
    (C) More than 10 minutes.
    (D) Less than 10 minutes.

( ) 2. By Matilda's calculations, how much money did her father make from selling five cars?
    (A) 4,333.5 pounds.
    (B) 4,335 pounds.
    (C) 4,033.5 pounds.
    (D) 4,303.5 pounds.

( ) 3. What made Mrs. Wormwood feel completely exhausted?
    (A) A lot of household chores.
    (B) The bingo games.
    (C) Her children.
    (D) Her sick husband.

## Further Discussion

1. What was five-year-old Matilda always forced to do? What were you usually told to do when you were five?

_____

_____

_____

_____

_____

_____

2. Why did Matilda's parents become comparatively civil to her? How long did the peace within the family last for?

_____

_____

_____

_____

_____

_____

3. Matilda showed a talent for math when her father asked her brother to add up the figures. Did Matilda receive praise from her father? Why or why not?

_____

_____

_____

_____

_____

_____

## Math Problems

Read and answer the following math problems by using math symbols in English!

I 2345

| Math Symbol | Meaning | Example |
|:---:|:---:|:---|
| + | plus | One **plus** one <u>is</u> / <u>equals</u> two. (1 + 1 = 2) |
| − | minus | Three **minus** one <u>is</u> / <u>equals</u> / <u>leaves</u> two. (3 − 1 = 2) |
| × | times | Four **times** three <u>is</u> / <u>equals</u> twelve. (4 × 3 = 12) |
| | multiplied by | Seven **multiplied by** two <u>is</u> / <u>equals</u> fourteen. (7 × 2 = 14) |
| ÷ | divided by | Ten **divided by** two <u>is</u> / <u>equals</u> five. (10 ÷ 2 = 5) |
| = | equal | Six plus one **equals** seven. (6 + 1 = 7) |

Mrs. Phelps sent Matilda three books for her birthday. Matilda also collected five cookbooks from her mother. How many books did Matilda have altogether?

Three plus five equals eight. Matilda had eight books altogether.

1. Michael has to make one hundred pancakes for his school event. He has already made twenty-five banana pancakes and seventy-three blueberry pancakes. How many pancakes does he still need to make?

2. A van costs twenty thousand dollars, and a truck costs ten thousand dollars. Mr. Wormwood sold two vans and one truck yesterday. How much did Mr. Wormwood get?

3. Mrs. Wormwood played bingo games twenty-one hours a week. Assuming that she played the same amount of hours each day, how many hours did she played bingo games each day?

# 5

# The Platinum-Blond Man
## Pages 56–65

## Word Power

1. foulness *n.* 卑鄙
2. dye *v.* 給…染色
3. tightrope-walker *n.* 走鋼索的人
4. peroxide *n.* 雙氧水
5. brainy *adj.* 聰明的

6. hair tonic *n.* 養髮液
7. stride *v.* 大步走
8. keep a straight face 板著臉
9. shriek *v.* 尖叫
10. disinfect *v.* 消毒

## Reading Comprehension

( ) 1. What color was Mrs. Wormwood's hair dyed?
   (A) Light brown.
   (B) Bright blue.
   (C) Platinum blonde.
   (D) Dark green.

( ) 2. According to Mr. Wormwood, what did "good strong hair" imply?
   (A) A healthy body.
   (B) A good strong brain underneath.
   (C) A kind heart.
   (D) A handsome face.

( ) 3. What did Matilda mix her father's hair tonic with?
   (A) Peanut butter and strawberry jam.
   (B) Cornflakes.
   (C) Elizabeth Arden face powder.
   (D) Platinum blonde hair-dye extra strong.

1. Why did Matilda invent another punishment for her father in this chapter? What punishment did Matilda give her father?

_____

_____

_____

_____

_____

_____

2. Mr. Wormwood always had two fried eggs on fried bread with three pork sausages, three strips of bacon, and some fried tomatoes for breakfast. How about you? What do you usually have for breakfast, and where do you eat it?

_____

_____

_____

_____

_____

_____

3. When Mr. Wormwood asked for help with his terrible hair color, who gave him advice? What advice did he/she give him?

_____

_____

_____

_____

_____

_____

## To Dye or Not to Dye, That's the Question

Have your family members or friends had any experiences of dyeing their hair? Interview a person with dyed hair about his or her opinions. Then write down his/her answers.

**1. What's your hair color now? Do you like it?**

- - - - - - - - - - - - - - - - - - - - - - - - - - - - - - - -

**2. What colors did you choose to dye your hair before? Why did you choose these colors?**

- - - - - - - - - - - - - - - - - - - - - - - - - - - - - - - -

**3. What does hair dyeing mean to you?**

- - - - - - - - - - - - - - - - - - - - - - - - - - - - - - - -

**4. If someone said you had your hair dyed to attract people's attention, how would you respond to him/her?**

- - - - - - - - - - - - - - - - - - - - - - - - - - - - - - - -

**5. Does dyeing damage your hair?**

Write down the pros (positive aspects) and cons (negative aspects) of hair dyeing.

# Pros

1. Getting new looks for a new start.

- - - - - - - - - - - - - - - - - - - - - - - - - - - - - - - - - - - - - - - -

# Cons

1. Causing dryness and allergic reactions such as a rash and irritable skin.

# 6

# Miss Honey
## Pages 66-81

## Word Power

1. commander *n.* 指揮官
2. bewilderment *n.* 困惑
3. tyrannical *adj.* 專橫的
4. menace *n.* 威脅
5. get on the wrong side of sb
   惹某人生氣

6. sink in 逐漸被完全理解
7. prodigy *n.* 神童
8. epicure *n.* 美食家
9. limerick *n.* 五行打油詩
10. astounded *adj.* 震驚的

## Reading Comprehension

(　) 1. Who is Miss Trunchbull?
   (A) Matilda's homeroom teacher.
   (B) Matilda's math teacher.
   (C) The head teacher of Matilda's school.
   (D) The librarian of Matilda's school.

(　) 2. What did Miss Honey's students have to know in a year's time?
   (A) The two-times table by heart.
   (B) How to use a calculator.
   (C) All the multiplication tables up to twelve.
   (D) A book of humorous poetry.

(　) 3. What is Miss Honey's first name?
   (A) Jenny.
   (B) Julie.
   (C) Genie.
   (D) Gina.

1. Do you remember your first day of elementary school? Try to describe the experience in a couple of sentences.

_____

_____

_____

_____

_____

_____

2. What kind of teacher is Miss Honey? What do you think a good teacher should be like? List at least three qualities that a good teacher should have.

_____

_____

_____

_____

_____

_____

3. According to Matilda, what's the difference between children and grown-ups? As a teenager, what do you think are the major differences between children and teenagers?

_____

_____

_____

_____

_____

_____

## Poem Writing

Matilda wrote a limerick which made Miss Honey blush and smile. A limerick is a comical poem consisting of five lines. The first, second, and fifth lines should have seven to ten syllables. They must have the same rhythm. The third and fourth lines should have five to seven syllables. They must rhyme with each other, too.

**A. Please mark the words that rhyme.**

| The Thing We All Ask About Jenny<br>by Matilda | There Was a Young Lady of Dorking<br>by Edward Lear |
|---|---|
| The thing we all ask about Jenny | There was a Young Lady of Dorking, |
| Is, "Surely there cannot be many | Who bought a large bonnet for walking; |
| Young girls in the place | But its color and size, |
| With so lovely a face?" | So bedazzled her eyes, |
| The answer to that is, "Not any!" | That she very soon went back to Dorking. |

**B. Write a limerick using the AABBA rhyme scheme on your own.**

| Title: | Rhyme Scheme |
|---|---|
|  | A |
|  | A |
|  | B |
|  | B |
|  | A |

# 7

## The Trunchbull
## Pages 82–89

## Word Power

1. ridiculous *adj.* 荒謬的
2. obstinate *adj.* 固執的
3. pillar of society 社會棟樑
4. off sb's rocker 某人發瘋

5. scorch *v.* 使⋯燒焦
6. unload . . . on sb 把⋯推卸給某人
7. wretched *adj.* 可憐的
8. viper *n.* 陰險的人；毒蛇

## Reading Comprehension

( ) 1. What did Miss Honey mention first when she described the amazing things Matilda had done to the Headmistress?
(A) Her reading ability.
(B) Her writing ability.
(C) Her superpower.
(D) Her talent for arithmetic.

( ) 2. What class did Miss Honey suggest placing Matilda in immediately?
(A) The class with the twelve-year-olds.
(B) The class with the ten-year-olds.
(C) Miss Plimsoll's top class.
(D) Miss Trunchbull's top class.

( ) 3. Did Miss Honey give up finding a way to help Matilda at the end of this chapter?
(A) Yes, she was too depressed to do anything about it.
(B) Yes, she decided to quit her teaching job.
(C) No, she was determined to find a way to help Matilda.
(D) No, she kept asking Miss Trunchbull for help.

1. Miss Honey excitedly headed for the Headmistress's study as soon as she finished the first class. What made her so excited?

   _____

   _____

   _____

   _____

   _____

   _____

2. Please describe Miss Trunchbull's facial and body features. Then try to describe one of your classmates and have the others guess who he/she is.

   _____

   _____

   _____

   _____

   _____

   _____

3. Why did Miss Trunchbull think that Mr. Wormwood was an excellent person and a pillar of society? In your opinion, what kind of person is considered a pillar of society? Please give an example to illustrate your point.

   _____

   _____

   _____

   _____

   _____

## Social Media

Miss Trunchbull had a rule in the school that all children remain in their own age groups regardless of their ability. Miss Honey found it unreasonable and wrote a social media post about this matter. Assuming that you were one of her followers, what would be your comment on it?

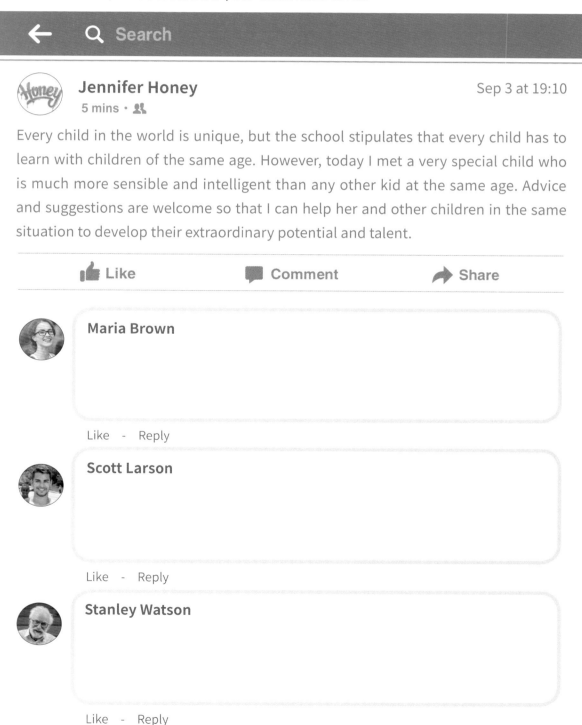

←    🔍 **Search**

**Jennifer Honey**            Sep 3 at 19:10
5 mins · 👥

Every child in the world is unique, but the school stipulates that every child has to learn with children of the same age. However, today I met a very special child who is much more sensible and intelligent than any other kid at the same age. Advice and suggestions are welcome so that I can help her and other children in the same situation to develop their extraordinary potential and talent.

👍 Like        💬 Comment        ➡ Share

**Maria Brown**

Like  -  Reply

**Scott Larson**

Like  -  Reply

**Stanley Watson**

Like  -  Reply

# 8

## The Parents
## Pages 90–100

## Word Power

1. geometry *n.* 幾何學
2. offspring *n.* 後代
3. tuition *n.* 一對一教學
4. get sth over with 完成必須做的討厭事
5. intrigue *v.* 使…感興趣
6. blue-stocking *n.* 才女
7. slave away 拼命工作
8. delinquent *n.* 不良青少年
9. in the flesh 當面
10. despise *v.* 輕視

## Reading Comprehension

(　　) 1. Why did Miss Honey feel confident about convincing Mr. and Mrs. Wormwood that their daughter was very special?
　　(A) She thought parents never belittle their kids' abilities.
　　(B) She assumed that Mrs. Wormwood was an intelligent woman.
　　(C) She heard that many people told Matilda's parents about Matilda's brilliance.
　　(D) She knew that Mr. and Mrs. Wormwood were so rich that they would pay extra money for Matilda's private tuition.

(　　) 2. What might be the time when Miss Honey arrived at the Wormwood's house?
　　(A) Between eight and nine o'clock.
　　(B) Around seven o'clock.
　　(C) Half past ten.
　　(D) Half past nine.

(　　) 3. Why did Miss Honey think that Matilda might be lying?
　　(A) Because Matilda said she didn't have a brilliant mind.
　　(B) Because Matilda said nobody taught her to multiply or read.
　　(C) Because Matilda said she liked Miss Trunchbull.
　　(D) Because Matilda said she had a happy family.

1. Without the support of the Headmistress, what did Miss Honey do to help Matilda develop her potential at school?

   _____

   _____

   _____

   _____

   _____

   _____

2. When Miss Honey communicated with Mr. Wormwood in a gentle and polite way, he seemed indifferent to her words. What did Miss Honey say later to give him a shock?

   _____

   _____

   _____

   _____

   _____

   _____

3. Miss Honey was called by three wrong names. What were those names? What is your name? If someone keeps getting your name wrong, how would you feel about it? What would you do to correct someone who screws up your name?

   _____

   _____

   _____

   _____

   _____

   _____

## Miss Honey's Emotional Range

The following are four events that Miss Honey has experienced. Try to draw Miss Honey's emotional range and describe her feelings during the events.

Hopeful
and
excited

Hopeless
and angry

| | | | |
|---|---|---|---|
| Talking to the Headmistress | Planning to talk with Matilda's parents | Talking to Mr. Wormwood | Talking to Mrs. Wormwood |

| Events | Miss Honey's Feelings |
|---|---|
| **Talking to the Headmistress** (p. 89) | Miss Honey felt depressed after the Headmistress rejected her suggestion that Matilda should be placed immediately in the top form. |
| **Planning to talk with Matilda's parents** | |
| **Talking to Mr. Wormwood** | |
| **Talking to Mrs. Wormwood** | |

# 9 Throwing the Hammer
## Pages 101–116

## Word Power

1. hammer *n.* 鏈球
2. adventurous *adj.* 喜歡冒險的
3. borstal *n.* 少年管訓所
4. regale sb with sth 以某事娛某人
5. squat *v.* 蹲
6. spike *v.* 刺穿

7. spellbound *adj.* 入迷的
8. culprit *n.* 罪魁禍首
9. be paralysed with fright
   被嚇得不知所措
10. scream blue murder 大聲抗議

## Reading Comprehension

( ) 1. If people had met Matilda casually, what would they have thought about her?
   (A) She was very sensible and quiet.
   (B) She was extraordinary.
   (C) She was good at literature and mathematics.
   (D) She was very intelligent.

( ) 2. What is true about "The Chokey"?
   (A) It is a very tall and wide cupboard.
   (B) The floor is about ten centimeters square.
   (C) Three of the walls are made of wood with broken glass.
   (D) The door has thousands of sharp nails sticking out of it.

( ) 3. Why was Hortensia put in The Chokey for the first time?
   (A) She poured Golden Syrup onto Miss Trunchbull's chair.
   (B) She ate an extra-large bag of potato crisps.
   (C) She told the newcomers about The Chokey.
   (D) She babbled like an idiot.

1. Why was Hortensia put in The Chokey for the second all-day stretch? Did Miss Trunchbull have any proof of her trick? Why did she still think Hortensia was the prime suspect?

_____

_____

_____

_____

_____

_____

2. What happened to Julius Rottwinkle when he was caught eating Liquorice Allsorts during the scripture class? Do you usually eat in class? What are the disadvantages of eating in class?

_____

_____

_____

_____

_____

_____

3. Why was Amanda Thripp thrown by Miss Trunchbull? If you were her, would you tell your parents about it? Why or why not? Give reasons to support your answer.

_____

_____

_____

_____

_____

_____

## Character Portraits as Animals

Imagine Crunchem Hall Primary School is a zoo. What animals come to your mind when you think of these characters? Try to find some textual evidence in the novel to support your answers.

| Characters | Animals | Reasons |
|---|---|---|
| **Matilda** | | |
| **Miss Trunchbull** | | |
| **Hortensia** | | |

What animal would you choose to represent your best friend? Why? Please state your reasons.

# 10

## Bruce Bogtrotter and the Cake
## Pages 117–133

### Word Power

1. get away with sth 做錯事而未被懲罰
2. raise a stink 公開抗議
3. outrageous *adj.* 嚇人的
4. go the whole hog 貫徹到底
5. riding crop *n.* 短馬鞭
6. wary *adj.* 謹慎的
7. crook *n.* 騙子
8. plead *v.* 辯解
9. shrivelled *adj.* 乾癟的
10. perseverance *n.* 堅持不懈

### Reading Comprehension

( ) 1. What would happen if Matilda told her parents about the pigtail story?
   (A) They would raise a terrific stink.
   (B) They would call her a liar.
   (C) They would encourage her to fight back.
   (D) They would ask her to keep it a secret.

( ) 2. Why did Miss Trunchbull order Bruce Bogtrotter to go up onto the platform?
   (A) He failed several subjects but refused to retake them.
   (B) He attacked the cook.
   (C) He stole a slice of her private chocolate cake.
   (D) He ate potato crisps in class.

( ) 3. What does "Go to blazes!" probably mean in the last paragraph of the chapter?
   (A) To ask someone to stand up.
   (B) To cheer someone up.
   (C) To tell someone to go away.
   (D) To warn someone of possible danger.

1. Matilda thought that Lavender's father might not believe her story. Have you had a similar experience? How did you feel when your parents didn't believe you? Share your story with your classmates.

_____

_____

_____

_____

_____

_____

2. Although Miss Trunchbull had no proof, what did she do to induce Bruce Bogtrotter to admit that he was the cake thief?

_____

_____

_____

_____

_____

_____

3. When Bruce Bogtrotter finished eating the 18-inch cake, all the other children cheered for him. What made Miss Trunchbull so furious, and what did she do to Bruce?

_____

_____

_____

_____

_____

_____

## Let's Make a Chocolate Cake!

Do you love chocolate cakes? Would you like to make one on your own? The following is a recipe for making a homemade chocolate cake.

**A. Find a chocolate cake recipe for 12 servings online and write down the ingredients.**

| Preparation Time | |
|---|---|
| Cooking Time | |
| **Ingredient** | **Amount** |
| | |
| | |
| | |
| | |
| | |
| | |
| | |
| | |
| | |
| | |
| | |
| | |
| | |

## B. Complete each step by using the words given below.

Step 1: <u>Preheat the oven to 180°C.</u>
(the oven / Preheat / 180°C. / to)

Step 2: _____
(all of / Mix / together. / the cake ingredients)

Step 3: _____
(some boiling water / to / the mixture. / Add)

Step 4: _____
(and bake / into the oven / Put the cake batter / for thirty minutes.)

Step 5: _____
(to cool. / and leave it / from the oven / Remove the cake)

Step 6: _____
(in a pan / until / Heat the chocolate and cream / they melt.)

Step 7: _____
(the cake / all over / with chocolate icing. / Ice)

# 11

# Lavender & The Weekly Test
# Pages 134–158

## Word Power

1. swot up 用功複習
2. scheming *adj.* 詭計多端的
3. bring sth off 完成某事
4. exploit *n.* 英勇的行為
5. go round the bend 發瘋

6. sewage worker *n.* 汙水處理工人
7. hesitation *n.* 遲疑不決
8. aloft *adv.* 在空中
9. wrench *v.* 猛拉；猛扯
10. a whopping great lie *n.* 彌天大謊

## Reading Comprehension

( ) 1. How often does the Headmistress take over Miss Honey's class?
  (A) Once a week.
  (B) Once a month.
  (C) Twice a week.
  (D) Twice a semester.

( ) 2. What must be prepared when the Headmistress enters the classroom?
  (A) A cup of hot tea and a glass of water.
  (B) A cup of coffee and a mug.
  (C) A pot of water and bottled water.
  (D) A jug of water and a glass.

( ) 3. What did the Headmistress ask Eric to spell?
  (A) Difficulty.
  (B) Ink.
  (C) What.
  (D) Write.

## Further Discussion

1. Nigel's father said that a bit of dirt never hurt anyone. Do you agree with him? Why or why not? Please give reasons to support your viewpoints.

   _____

   _____

   _____

   _____

   _____

   _____

2. Miss Honey taught her students a magic method to recite the spelling of words. What was it? Do you have any magic method to learn difficult words?

   _____

   _____

   _____

   _____

   _____

   _____

3. Why did Miss Trunchbull accuse Mr. Wormwood of being a crook? If you were Miss Trunchbull, what would you do when you found out you were ripped off?

   _____

   _____

   _____

   _____

   _____

   _____

## Character Log

Find and write down each character's basic information, physical appearance or personality traits. Then, draw a picture of each character.

### *Matilda*
- an extraordinary, sensitive, and brilliant girl
- is fond of reading
- taught herself to read at three

### *Miss Honey*

### *Lavender*

### *Nigel Hicks*

# 12

## The First Miracle &
## The Second Miracle
## Pages 159–176

## Word Power

1. the bane of sth 某物的剋星
2. be round the twist 發瘋
3. not have the faintest idea 根本不知道
4. own up 坦白
5. behind bars 在監獄裡

6. tip sth over 使某物翻倒
7. vouch for sth 為某事擔保
8. flinch *v.* 退縮
9. bottle up 抑制
10. confide in sb 向某人傾訴

## Reading Comprehension

( ) 1. What was Miss Trunchbull's idea of a perfect school?
   (A) A school without children.
   (B) A school without teachers.
   (C) A school without tests.
   (D) A school without insects.

( ) 2. When Miss Trunchbull poured some water into the glass, what came out of her water jug?
   (A) A lizard.
   (B) A newt.
   (C) A crocodile.
   (D) A snake.

( ) 3. Why did Matilda get furious when she was accused of playing a trick on Miss Trunchbull?
   (A) Matilda knew who had done it but that person didn't admit it.
   (B) Miss Honey kept silent instead of coming to her rescue.
   (C) Miss Trunchbull cursed her for her bad attitude.
   (D) Matilda was blamed for a crime that she hadn't committed.

1. In what situation did Matilda perform the first miracle? How did she perform it?

_____

_____

_____

_____

_____

_____

2. Who did Matilda think of when she wanted to confide in someone? What might be the reason that Matilda chose him or her to confide in? If you want to share your secrets, who do you usually share them with? Why?

_____

_____

_____

_____

_____

_____

3. What was Matilda's second miracle, and how did Miss Honey react to it?

_____

_____

_____

_____

_____

 **Magic Power**

In the story, Matilda possesses an incredible magic power. If you could be granted a magic power, what magic power would you want to get? What could you do with that power?

### Mind Reading

If I were able to read people's minds, I would know if they were telling the truth or lying to me.

If you were granted with one magic power to go into the novel with it, what power would you choose? How would you help Matilda and Miss Honey with it?

# 13

## Miss Honey's Cottage
## Pages 177–192

### Word Power

1. greengrocer *n.* 蔬果商
2. butcher *n.* 肉商
3. proceedings *n.* 一系列事件
4. precocious *adj.* 早熟的
5. hedge *n.* 樹籬

6. profoundly *adv.* 深刻地
7. margarine *n.* 人造鮮奶油
8. delicacy *n.* 微妙性
9. perch *v.* 坐在…上
10. round sth off 使某事圓滿結束

### Reading Comprehension

(     ) 1. Why did Miss Honey calm Matilda down?
    (A) Miss Honey wanted to figure the proceedings out as soon as possible.
    (B) Matilda kept trying to topple tables and chairs immediately.
    (C) Matilda was too excited, thinking she could move everything by staring at it.
    (D) Miss Honey was fascinated by the mysterious forces in Matilda's eyes.

(     ) 2. According to Miss Honey, what does "a precocious child" refer to?
    (A) A child who can move something without touching it.
    (B) A child who shows amazing intelligence at an early age.
    (C) A child who likes reading very much.
    (D) A child who is very good at math.

(     ) 3. Where did Miss Honey live?
    (A) She lived in a spacious apartment.
    (B) She lived in a grand villa.
    (C) She lived in a log cabin.
    (D) She lived in an old red-brick cottage.

1. Try to describe the appearance of Miss Honey's house. Do you want to live in that kind of house? Why or why not?

_____

_____

_____

_____

_____

2. When walking on the path to the cottage, Miss Honey recited a poem which made Matilda think of an illustration from books of fairy tales. Try to match the key words from the poem with the fairy tales.

_____

_____

_____

_____

_____

_____

3. What was Matilda's reaction when she became suddenly aware of the situation that Miss Honey's living conditions were not as good as hers? If you were Matilda, what would you do to help Miss Honey?

_____

_____

_____

_____

_____

## A House for Miss Honey

Imagine you are an interior designer, and you are assigned the task of helping Miss Honey design her new flat. The following are two kinds of floor plans: one is an open floor plan and the other is a closed floor plan. In your opinion, which one meets Miss Honey's needs and tastes? State your reasons and use your imagination to design the flat.

A: Open Floor Plan

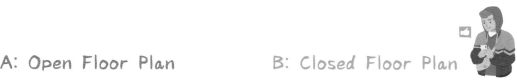

B: Closed Floor Plan

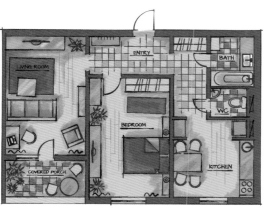

_____
_____
_____
_____
_____
_____
_____
_____
_____
_____
_____
_____
_____
_____

# 14

# Miss Honey's Story
# Pages 193-205

## Word Power

1. probe *v.* 追問，探究
2. rigid *adj.* 僵直的
3. knock sb out of sth
   使某人喪失某種素質
4. be tucked away 隱藏
5. guardian *n.* 監護人

6. sane *adj.* 心智健全的
7. pluck up the courage 鼓起勇氣
8. be better off 境況更好
9. next of kin *n.* 直系親屬
10. forgery *n.* 偽造品

## Reading Comprehension

( ) 1. According to Matilda, which of the following was **NOT** a negative aspect of living in a simple way as Miss Honey did?
   (A) It made house cleaning a much easier job.
   (B) It saved a lot of laundry.
   (C) Miss Honey didn't have to buy lots of food to fill up a fridge.
   (D) Miss Honey could save half of her income every month.

( ) 2. How many years had Miss Honey lived in the cottage?
   (A) Four years.
   (B) Three years.
   (C) Two years.
   (D) One year.

( ) 3. Why didn't Miss Honey quit her job and live on unemployment money?
   (A) She had a strong passion for teaching.
   (B) She was not eligible for unemployment benefits.
   (C) She thought the benefits should be given to those in need.
   (D) Her father left her a large inheritance.

## Further Discussion

1. Why didn't Miss Honey talk to anyone about her problems? Why did she decide to tell Matilda about her miserable childhood? If you were Miss Honey, would you tell others about your suffering?

_____

_____

_____

_____

_____

_____

2. Why did Miss Honey's father invite her aunt to come and live with them? Was there someone who took care of you when you were young? How did you feel about it?

_____

_____

_____

_____

_____

_____

3. How did Miss Honey budget her pocket money? How do you do this?

_____

_____

_____

_____

_____

_____

 **Music Appreciation**

Miss Honey led a tough life. In order to escape from her aunt, she managed to live alone on a tight budget. Please choose a song that best describes Miss Honey and answer the following questions.

**1. What song do you want to choose for Miss Honey? Why?**

**2. What does the song try to convey?**

**3. What is your favorite part of the song?**

**4. When do you listen to the song?**

# 15
# The Names & The Practice
## Pages 206~214

## Word Power

1. come along 快點
2. take charge of 負責
3. call out 大聲叫出
4. essential *adj.* 必要的
5. ethereal *adj.* 超凡的
6. summon up 積聚
7. trigger *n.* 扳機
8. colossal *adj.* 巨大的

## Reading Comprehension

(　) 1. Why did Matilda want to go home after hearing Miss Honey's story?
　　 (A) It was very late.
　　 (B) Her mother would worry about her.
　　 (C) She wanted to think about all the things she had heard.
　　 (D) She had much homework to do.

(　) 2. What did Matilda promise Miss Honey?
　　 (A) She promised to forget everything she had heard in Miss Honey's cottage.
　　 (B) She promised to take revenge on Miss Trunchbull.
　　 (C) She promised not to reveal Miss Honey's secret.
　　 (D) She promised not to do experiments with her magic power.

(　) 3. What did Miss Honey's father call her aunt?
　　 (A) Magnus.
　　 (B) Jenny.
　　 (C) Trunchbull.
　　 (D) Agatha.

## Further Discussion

1. Who is Miss Honey's aunt, and how did the aunt treat Miss Honey after the death of her father? How would you feel about it, and what would you do if you were little Jenny?

_____

_____

_____

_____

_____

_____

2. What did Matilda choose to practice her power with? How did she practice with it?

_____

_____

_____

_____

_____

_____

3. As the saying goes, "Practice makes perfect." Matilda felt a sense of achievement after succeeding in developing her supernatural ability. Have you ever practiced hard for something and eventually enjoyed the fruits of your labor? Please share your experience.

_____

_____

_____

_____

_____

_____

## Character Word Cloud

Come up with at least ten personality traits for Miss Honey, and find the textual evidence to support your answers. Then, use these traits to create a word cloud portraying this character, or you may include a picture, image, or symbol that you think can represent her.

| Personality Traits | Textual Evidence |
|---|---|
| mild / quiet | Miss Honey never raised her voice and was adored by every kid under her care. (pp. 66–67) |
|  |  |
|  |  |
|  |  |
|  |  |
|  |  |
|  |  |

# 16

# The Third Miracle
# Pages 215–226

## Word Power

1. smart-aleck *adj.* 自作聰明的
2. get the better of sb 擊敗某人
3. apprehensive *adj.* 擔憂的
4. rolling-pin *n.* 擀麵棍
5. impertinent *adj.* 無禮的

6. somersault *n.* 筋斗
7. prostrate *adj.* 一蹶不振的
8. out cold 不省人事的
9. elated *adj.* 興高采烈的
10. matron *n.* 護士

## Reading Comprehension

(　) 1. What did Miss Trunchbull test the kids on when she took the class on Thursday afternoon?
 (A) Addition.
 (B) Subtraction.
 (C) Multiplication.
 (D) Division.

(　) 2. Who was the first one to notice the moving chalk?
 (A) Eric.
 (B) Miss Honey.
 (C) Miss Trunchbull.
 (D) Nigel.

(　) 3. What was Miss Trunchbull's reaction as soon as she saw the chalk writing something on its own?
 (A) She ran out of the classroom immediately.
 (B) She was shocked and wanted to find out who did it.
 (C) She accused Matilda of being the mastermind behind the trick.
 (D) She yelled at Miss Honey.

1. What was the third miracle that happened in this chapter? Do you think Miss Honey knew who performed it? Why?

_____

_____

_____

_____

_____

_____

2. What did the message on the blackboard tell Miss Trunchbull to do? Do you think Miss Trunchbull would follow the instructions? Why?

_____

_____

_____

_____

_____

_____

3. Why did Nigel pour water over Miss Trunchbull's head? If you see someone faint, what would you do to help him/her?

_____

_____

_____

_____

_____

_____

## Reverse Spelling Game

SCAN ME

"TACOCAT" — Parry Gripp

In the story, Miss Honey asked Miss Trunchbull whether she could spell simple words like *wrong* backwards. In fact, some English words can read the same when people read them forward or backwards. These words are called palindromes, and the American rock quartet Tacocat is an example.

**A. Find at least six words that read the same forward and backwards.**




**B. The following are five reverse pairs, which are read one way forward and the other way backwards. Think about the interesting relation between the two and use each pair to make a sentence to describe the characters or events in *Matilda*.**

1. "Desserts" spelled backwards is "stressed."

→ Bruce loved eating **desserts** like chocolate cakes when he felt stressed.
_____

2. "Evil" spelled backwards is "live."

→ _____
_____

3. "Trap" spelled backwards is "part."

→ _____
_____

4. "Pot" spelled backwards is "top."

→ _____
_____

5. "Saw" spelled backwards is "was."

→ _____
_____

# 17

## A New Home
## Pages 227-240

## Word Power

1. deputy head *n.* 副校長
2. do a bunk 溜走；不告而別
3. solicitor *n.* 律師
4. testament *n.* 遺囑
5. late *adj.* 已故的

6. be off the mark 不正確
7. beat it 走開
8. tip sb off 向某人告密
9. not care tuppence 毫不在乎
10. boot *n.* 後車箱

## Reading Comprehension

( ) 1. Who was Mr. Trilby?
    (A) The school counselor.
    (B) The school security guard.
    (C) The school social worker.
    (D) The vice principal of the school.

( ) 2. Where did Mr. Wormwood plan to go?
    (A) He would move to Spain.
    (B) He would take a trip to France.
    (C) He would immigrate to the United States.
    (D) He would flee to Australia.

( ) 3. What was Mrs. Wormwood's response after she heard Miss Honey's request?
    (A) She rejected her request and insisted that Matilda should go with them.
    (B) She granted her request and let her have Matilda.
    (C) Miss Honey's request left her speechless with shock.
    (D) She was mad at Miss Honey for making such a rude request.

1. According to Miss Honey's guess, why couldn't Matilda tip anything over with her eyes anymore? How did Matilda feel about it?

_____

_____

_____

_____

_____

_____

2. What might be the reason that Mr. Wormwood had to leave his hometown?

_____

_____

_____

_____

_____

_____

3. After the car left, Matilda and Miss Honey hugged each other silently. In your opinion, what was on their minds at that moment?

_____

_____

_____

_____

_____

_____

## Continue the Story

After Mr. and Mrs. Wormwood left, what might happen in the next chapter? Please choose a possible ending from the following three and continue the story.

The police asked Matilda about her father's whereabouts and Matilda said . . . .

**1**

Mr. Wormwood was arrested at the airport and . . . .

**2**

The Wormwood family fled to Spain . . . .

**3**

_____
_____
_____
_____
_____
_____
_____
_____
_____
_____
_____
_____
_____
_____
_____
_____
_____
_____
_____

# Overall Review

Congratulations on finishing *Matilda*. Now imagine you are a renowned book critic, and your fans are waiting for your review of this book.

My Rating:

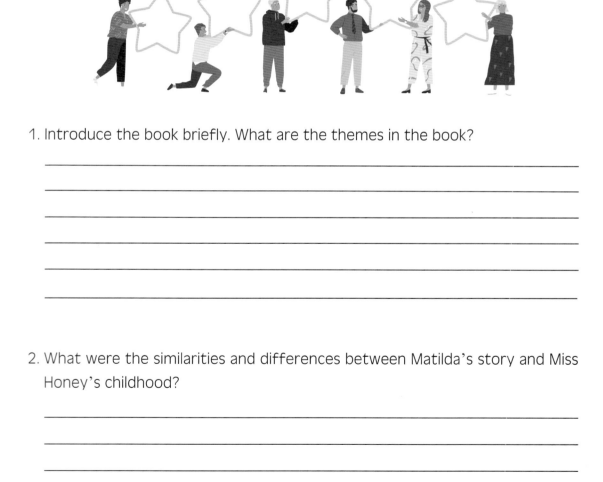

1. Introduce the book briefly. What are the themes in the book?

_____
_____
_____
_____
_____
_____

2. What were the similarities and differences between Matilda's story and Miss Honey's childhood?

_____
_____
_____
_____
_____
_____

3. What is your favorite part in the book? Why?

_____

_____

_____

_____

_____

_____

4. What are the moral lessons in the book? What did Roald Dahl want to convey to us?

_____

_____

_____

_____

_____

_____

5. Who would you recommend this book to? Why?

_____

_____

_____

_____

_____

_____

◆ Wonder 解讀攻略

戴逸群 編著／Joseph E. Schier 審閱
Lexile 藍思分級：790

☞ 議題：品德教育、生命教育、家庭教育、閱讀素養

◆ Harry Potter and the Sorcerer's Stone
解讀攻略

戴逸群 主編／簡嘉妤 編著／Ian Fletcher 審閱
Lexile 藍思分級：880

☞ 議題：品德教育、家庭教育、多元文化、閱讀素養

◆ Love, Simon 解讀攻略

戴逸群 主編／林冠瑋 編著／Ian Fletcher 審閱
Lexile 藍思分級：640

☞ 議題：性別平等、人權教育、多元文化、閱讀素養

## Answer Key

### Lesson 1
Reading Comprehension
1. (A)   2. (C)   3. (D)

### Lesson 2
Reading Comprehension
1. (A)   2. (C)   3. (C)

### Lesson 3
Reading Comprehension
1. (C)   2. (B)   3. (A)

### Lesson 4
Reading Comprehension
1. (D)   2. (D)   3. (B)

Math Problems
1. Two pancakes.
2. Fifty thousand dollars.
3. Three hours.

### Lesson 5
Reading Comprehension
1. (C)   2. (B)   3. (D)

### Lesson 6
Reading Comprehension
1. (C)   2. (C)   3. (A)

Poem Writing
A. Jenny / many / (place) / (face) / any
Dorking / walking / (size) / (eyes) /
Dorking

### Lesson 7
Reading Comprehension
1. (D)   2. (C)   3. (C)

### Lesson 8
Reading Comprehension
1. (A)   2. (D)   3. (B)

### Lesson 9
Reading Comprehension
1. (A)   2. (D)   3. (A)

### Lesson 10
Reading Comprehension
1. (B)   2. (C)   3. (C)

Let's Make a Chocolate Cake
B. 2. Mix all of the cake ingredients together.
   3. Add some boiling water to the mixture.
   4. Put the cake batter into the oven and bake for thirty minutes.
   5. Remove the cake from the oven and leave it to cool.
   6. Heat the chocolate and cream in a pan until they melt.
   7. Ice the cake all over with the chocolate icing.

### Lesson 11
Reading Comprehension
1. (A)   2. (D)   3. (C)

### Lesson 12
Reading Comprehension
1. (A)   2. (B)   3. (D)

### Lesson 13
Reading Comprehension
1. (C)   2. (B)   3. (D)

## Lesson 14

Reading Comprehension

1. (B)   2. (C)   3. (A)

## Lesson 15

Reading Comprehension

1. (C)   2. (C)   3. (D)

## Lesson 16

Reading Comprehension

1. (C)   2. (D)   3. (B)

## Lesson 17

Reading Comprehension

1. (D)   2. (A)   3. (B)